## EGMONT
*We bring stories to life*

First published in Great Britain 2014
by Egmont UK Limited
The Yellow Building, 1 Nicholas Road, London W11 4AN
www.egmont.co.uk

Text and illustrations copyright © Angie Morgan 2014
Angie Morgan has asserted her moral rights.
All photographs courtesy of Shutterstock.

ISBN 978 1 4052 6677 2 (Paperback)
ISBN 978 1 7803 1485 3 (Ebook)

A CIP catalogue record for this title
is available from the British Library.

Wildlife is **foxes** and **squirrels**
and **frogs** and **fish** and **birds**
and **creepy-crawlies**
and **toads** and **spiders** and
**bees** and lots and lots more.

**Wildlife**

For Luke, who used to be shouty
but who's all grown up now — A.M.

Can you spot
the ladybird
throughout
the book?

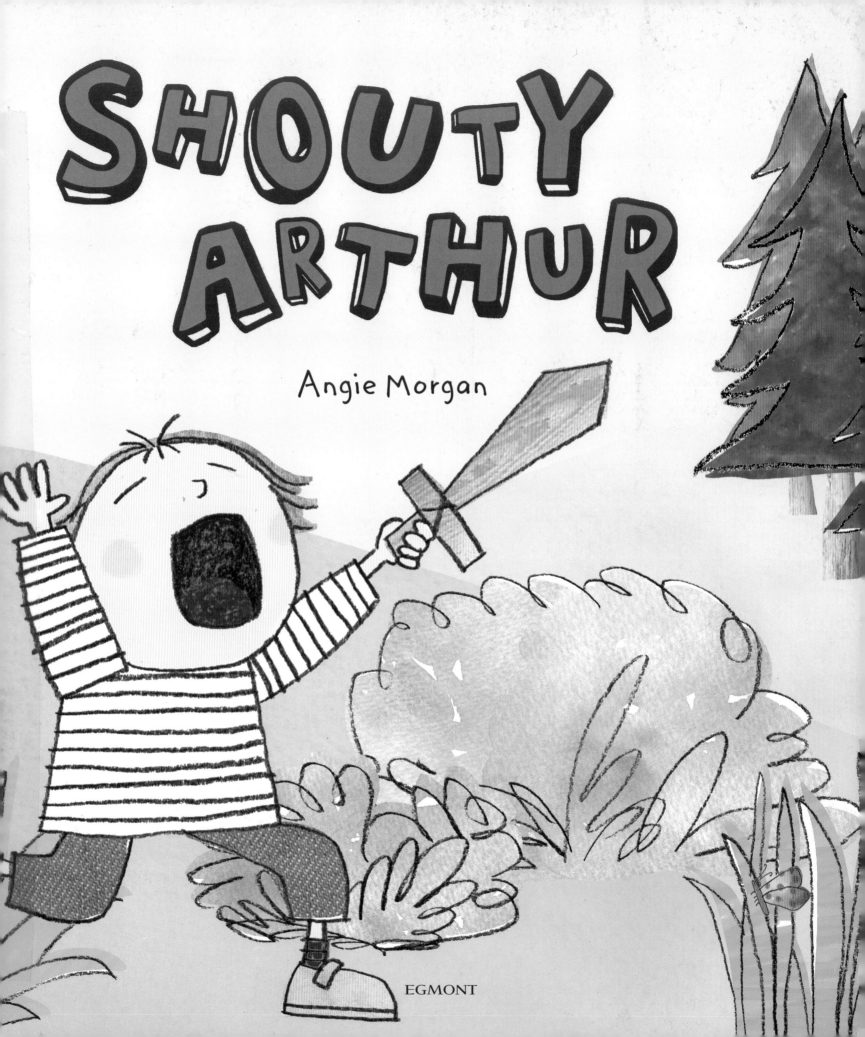

Edith was reading her new book.

"What are you reading, Edith?" asked her little brother, Arthur.

"Go away, Arthur," said Edith.

"Is it very interesting?" he asked.

"Yes," said Edith. "It's all about wildlife."

"What's wildlife?" asked Arthur.     "Well," said Edith, "it's . . .

...rabbits

...and birds

...and foxes

...and ladybirds

...and beetles

...and bees

...and owls

...and dragonflies

...and frogs

...and fish

...and deer."

"Wow," said Arthur. "Can we see some?"

"Only if you are VERY quiet," said Edith. "Wildlife doesn't like loud noises."

"Don't worry," said Arthur, "I'll be as quiet as a mouse."

So Edith took her book and packed some lunch, and Arthur took his sword and they both set off to find some wildlife.

KA-POW!

They didn't see much.

"We haven't seen any wildlife yet, Edith!" shouted Arthur.

"That's because you're too shouty," said Edith. "You promised to be quiet."

"Being quiet is very hard," said Arthur.

"I'll read from my book," said Edith. "It tells you where all the animals live."

"Rabbits live in burrows under the ground. Rabbit holes are in banks and hedgerows," she read.

Wildlife is **foxes** and **squirrels** and **frogs** and **fish** and **birds** and **creepy-crawlies** and **toads** and **spiders** and **bees** and lots and lots more.

Wildlife

Wildlife

"COME OUT, YOU OLD RABBITS!"

shouted Arthur.

But there were no rabbits to be seen.

Wildlife is **foxes** and **squirrels** and **frogs** and **fish** and **birds** and **creepy-crawlies** and **toads** and **spiders** and **bees** and lots and lots more.

"Frogs live in ponds and damp places," continued Edith.

# "COME OUT, YOU OLD FROGS!"

shouted Arthur.

But there were no frogs to be seen.

"Squirrels live in nests high up in the branches of trees," read Edith.

Wildlife is **foxes** and **squirrels** and **frogs** and **fish** and **birds** and **creepy-crawlies** and **toads** and **spiders** and **bees** and lots and lots more.

Wildlife

"COME OUT, YOU OLD SQUIRRELS!"
shouted Arthur.

But there were no squirrels either.

"Edith, I'm getting a bit tired and hungry now," said Arthur.

So Edith gave Arthur
his lunch – and after
he had eaten it . . .

he curled up and had a little sleep.

Edith and the wildlife
enjoyed the peace and quiet.

After a while Arthur woke up.

"It's getting late," said Edith.
"We should be going home."

"Wildlife is a bit boring, isn't it, Edith?"
shouted Arthur as they walked home.
"There were no rabbits and no frogs
and not even one single squirrel.
There was nothing to see at all."

At bedtime Arthur was a bit glum.
"What are you reading, Edith?" he asked.

"I'm reading about nocturnal animals," said Edith.
"They're animals that come out at night."

Nocturnal Wildlife

Owls and moths
and bats and foxes
and toads and voles
and lots and lots more.

"It's night-time now,"
said Arthur. "Could we
go into the garden and
see some, please?"

"You must promise not to be shouty," said Edith.

"I will try my VERY hardest," promised Arthur.

And Arthur did try VERY hard not to be shouty.

But he only managed it for a VERY little while . . .

Arthur's Hints on

# HOW TO WATCH WILDLIFE

1. Be very QUIET
2. Don't jump about
3. Be POLITE
4. Always take a SNACK
(watching wildlife is very TIRING
and it makes you HUNGRY)